The Pout-Pout Fish

in the Big-Big Dark

Deborah Diesen

Pictures by Dan Hanna

SCHOLASTIC INC.
New York Toronto London Auckland
Sydney Mexico City New Delhi Hong Kong

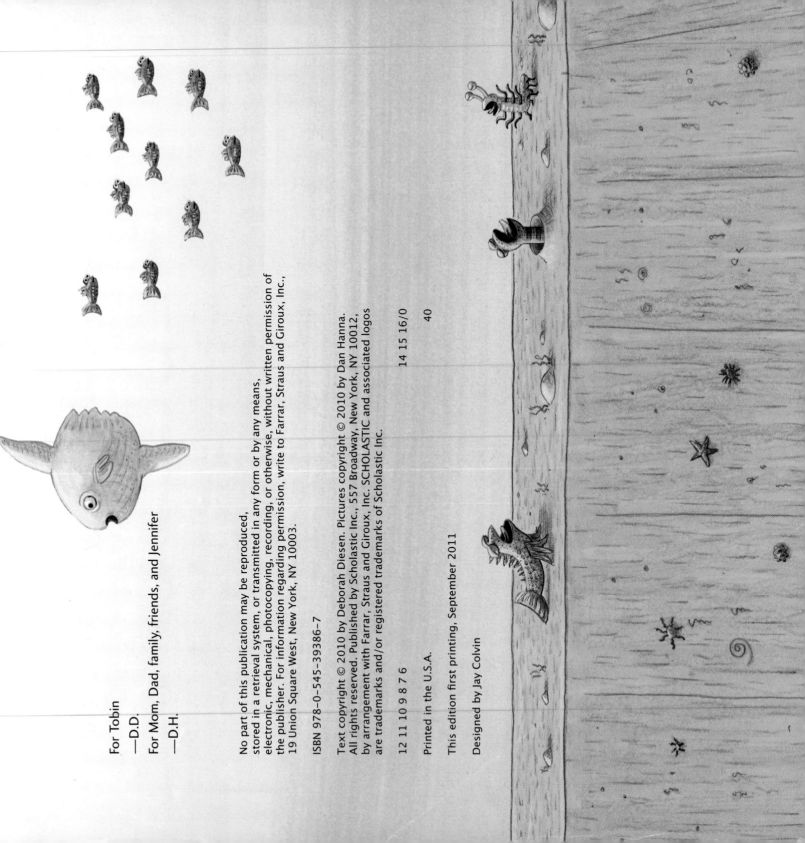

For Tobin
—D.D.

For Mom, Dad, family, friends, and Jennifer
—D.H.

ISBN 978-0-545-39386-7

12 11 10 9 8 7 6   14 15 16/0

                                     40

Printed in the U.S.A.

This edition first printing, September 2011

Designed by Jay Colvin

A doozie of a drowsy
Made Ms. Clam yawn.
Then a big current *whooshed*
And her pearl was GONE!

Mr. Fish swam forth.
"Ms. Clam, don't weep!
I will find your pearl—
That's a promise I'll keep!"

He swooped through the water,
Swishing close to the sand,
And he eyed every inch
Of the busy bottom land.

He found a mucky marble
Where he thought the pearl might be.

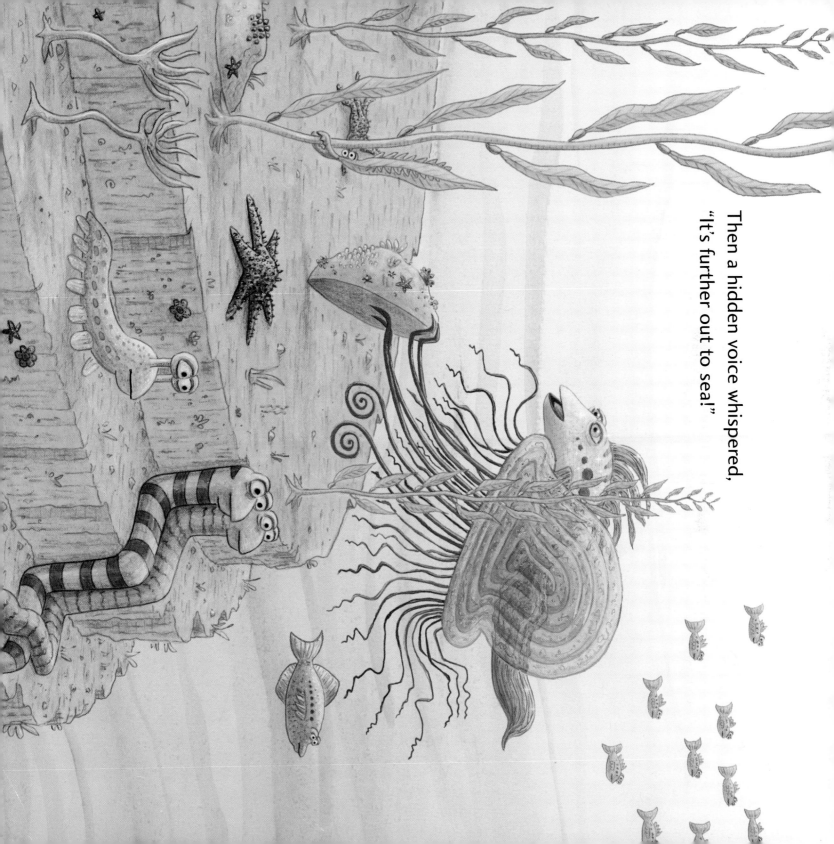

Then a hidden voice whispered,
"It's further out to sea!"

So he swam a little deeper,
Where the light grew dimmer.
As his heart flit-fluttered,
Mr. Fish grew grimmer.

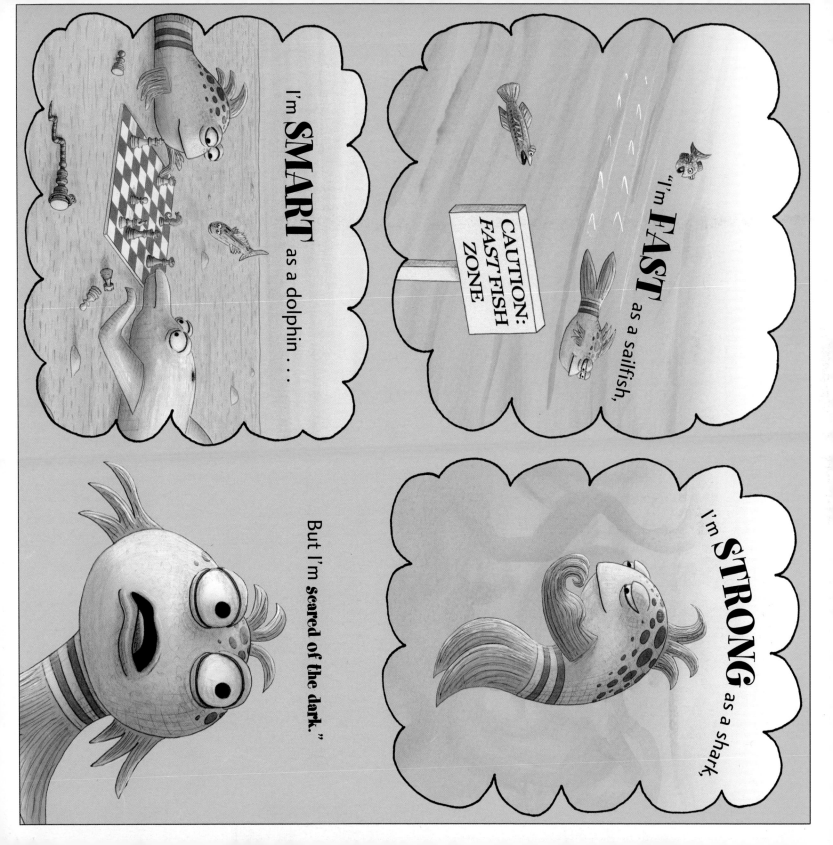

He kept on searching
All along the ocean floor,

Through a reef, through a wreck,
Swimming far from the shore.

Mr. Fish felt a pout-pout
Poach on his hope.

Then the whisper from before
Said, "It's down beyond the slope!"

So he swam a little deeper,
Where the light grew dimmer.
As his heart flit-fluttered,
Mr. Fish grew grimmer.

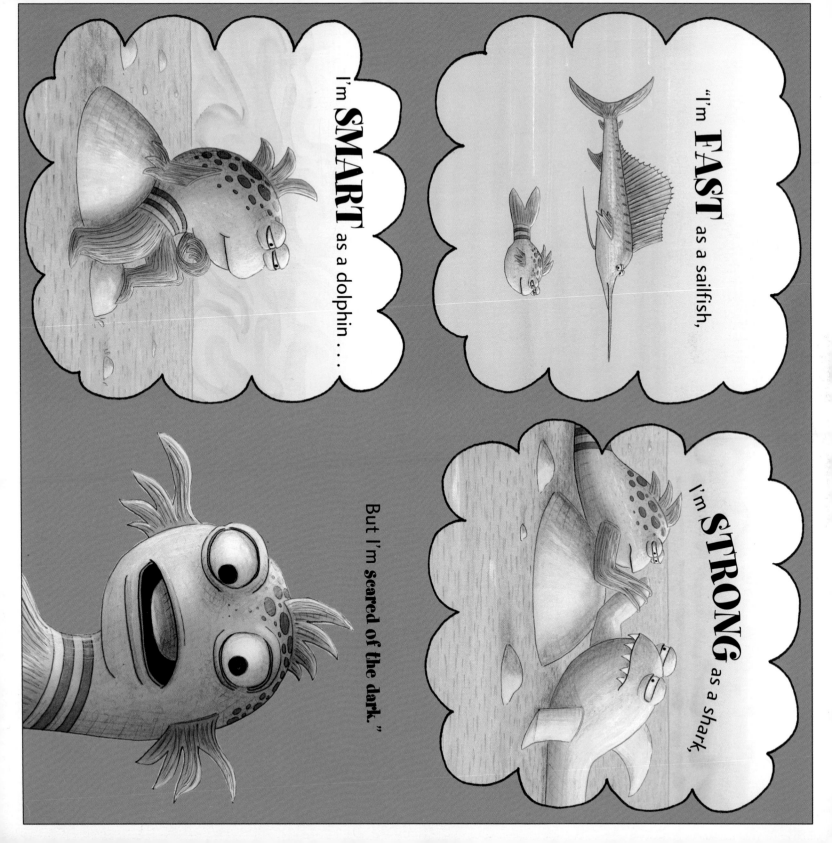

A whirl of wriggly worms
Made a search-team swirl,
And they helped with the hunt
For the yawn-gone pearl.

But nothing was discovered.
Mr. Fish felt despair!
Then that soft voice whispered,
"In the trench—check there."

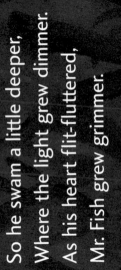

So he swam a little deeper,
Where the light grew dimmer.
As his heart flit-fluttered,
Mr. Fish grew grimmer.

"I'm **FAST** as a sailfish,

I'm **SMART** as a dolphin . . .

I'm **STRONG** as a shark,

But I'm **SCARED OF THE DARK!**"

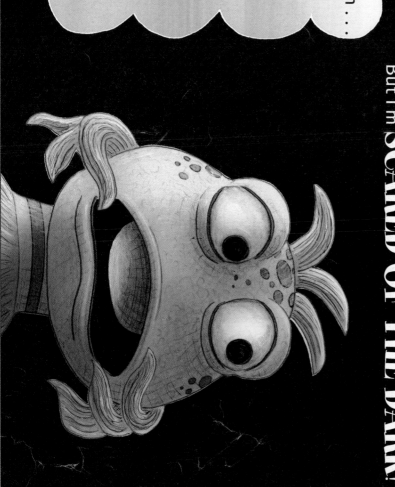

"I *won't* keep swimming
In this heap-deep black!
I know I made a promise,
But this fish is headin' back!"

Then a whisper, now familiar,
Whisked away his dread.
"You can *do* it, Mr. Fish,"
Her sweet voice said.

Though there wasn't any light,
Not the smallest, slim glimmer,
Mr. Fish felt braver . . .

Cheered on by Miss Shimmer:

"Two are **FASTER** than a sailfish,

Two are **STRONGER** than a shark,

Two are **SMARTER** than a dolphin . . .

Two are **BIGGER** than the dark!"

So they swam down together,
Holding fin to fin,
When suddenly,
Amazingly . . .

LIGHT
SHONE
IN!

Mr. Fish said, "Yes!"
Miss Shimmer shouted, "Yay!"
"There's Ms. Clam's pearl!
Hooray! Hoo-*ray*!!!"

They **SMOOCHED** Mr. Lantern.

Then they smiled as they swam,
Weaving back through the water
To a happy Ms. Clam.

The whole gang gathered,
Feeling glorious and proud,
And they swam in a circle
As they sang out loud:

"The ocean is wide,
And the ocean is deep,
But *friends help friends*—
That's a promise we keep."

 We are bigger,

Yes, BIGGER,

Always big,